Éric Veillé • Pauline Martin

THE
BUREAU OF
MISPLACED

Kids Can Press

I accidentally misplaced my dad this morning.

I ran outside to look for him.
I asked a man if he had seen my dad.

"It just so happens that I work at the Bureau of
Misplaced Dads," he said. "Come with me. With any
luck, your father will be there waiting for you …

At least 20 or 30 dads wander in every day.
They're usually in fairly good condition.

If they're lucky, their kids come to fetch them the same day ...

But we have dads here who've been waiting around since the dawn of time.

We give the dads who cry cookies and juice,
and it seems to help a bit.

The dads in striped sweaters
hang out in the Ping-Pong room.

And the bearded dads chew
mint-flavored bubble gum.

Once a year, we release a few dads back into the wild. Just for fun.

The dads aren't allowed to play with the crocodiles …

But otherwise, they can pretty much do as they please.

The older dads play checkers. (And the kids who come to claim them are often quite old themselves.)

"I've seen tons of dads over the years.
What does yours look like?"
"Well, he's *my* dad!"
"Of course. He's probably over here — is this him?"
"NO!"

"You know, if you don't find him, you could always adopt another one. Let's see who I have for you:

A dad from Strasbourg, wearing his daughter's bonnet

A Super Dad

A colorfully dressed dad

A clueless dad

A dad with crumbs in his mustache

A dad who always looks like he's just gotten out of bed

A dad named Michael

A dad who smells like the mountains …

"No, No, NO! I want *my* dad. He knows me, and he's the one who drives me to school."
"Ah. Well, in that case, I'm afraid I can't help you."

"Oh! I know where my dad is! I remember now.
I asked him to pretend he was a coat rack!"

"I see. Let's get you home quickly, then. Go down this hall. You'll see an old dog. Next to the dog is a ladder — climb up. It's a shortcut."

"DAD!"

"I've been waiting for you to find me!"

First published in France under the title *Le bureau des papas perdus* © Actes Sud, Paris, 2013.

Text and illustrations © 2013 Actes Sud

English translation © 2015 Kids Can Press
English translation by Yvette Ghione

Kids Can Press acknowledges the financial support of the Government of Ontario, through the Ontario Media Development Corporation's Ontario Book Initiative.

Published in Canada by
Kids Can Press Ltd.
25 Dockside Drive
Toronto, ON M5A 0B5

Published in the U.S. by
Kids Can Press Ltd.
2250 Military Road
Tonawanda, NY 14150

www.kidscanpress.com

The artwork in this book was rendered digitally.
The text is set in Caecilia.

English edition edited by Katie Scott

This book is smyth sewn casebound.
Manufactured in Shenzhen, China, in 3/2015 by C & C Offset.

CM 15 0 9 8 7 6 5 4 3 2 1

Library and Archives Canada Cataloguing in Publication

Veillé, Éric, 1976–
[Bureau des papas perdus. English]
    The bureau of misplaced dads / written by Éric Veillé ; illustrated by Pauline Martin.

Translation of: Le Bureau des papas perdus.
ISBN 978-1-77138-238-0 (bound)

    I. Martin, Pauline, 1975–, illustrator II. Title. III. Title: Bureau des papas perdus. English.

PZ7.V44Bu 2015   j843'.92   C2014-906851-4

For Juana and Émile
P. M.

Kids Can Press is a ℓℴrus™ Entertainment company